Coolest Dance Crazes

Larry Swartz • Indrani Margolin

Series Editor
Jeffrey D. Wilhelm

Much thought, debate, and research went into choosing and ranking the 10 items in each book in this series. We realize that everyone has his or her own opinion of what is most significant, revolutionary, amazing, deadly, and so on. As you read, you may agree with our choices, or you may be surprised — and that's the way it should be!

an imprint of
SCHOLASTIC
www.scholastic.com/librarypublishing

A Rubicon book published in association with Scholastic Inc.

 Rubicon © 2008 Rubicon Publishing Inc.
www.rubiconpublishing.com

All rights reserved. No part of this publication may be reproduced, stored in a database or retrieval system, distributed, or transmitted in any form or by any means, electronic, mechanical, photocopying, recording, or otherwise, without the prior written permission of Rubicon Publishing Inc.

 is a trademark of The 10 Books

SCHOLASTIC and associated logos and designs are trademarks and/or registered trademarks of Scholastic Inc.

Associate Publishers: Kim Koh, Miriam Bardswich
Project Editor: Amy Land
Editor: Dawna McKinnon
Creative Director: Jennifer Drew
Project Manager/Designer: Jeanette MacLean
Graphic Designers: Katherine Park, Julie Whatman

The publisher gratefully acknowledges the following for permission to reprint copyrighted material in this book.

Every reasonable effort has been made to trace the owners of copyrighted material and to make due acknowledgment. Any errors or omissions drawn to our attention will be gladly rectified in future editions.

"U.S. hears the beat of Macarena dance craze" (excerpt) by Kathleen Barnes. Permission courtesy of CNN.

"The hustle is still hot on Detroit dance scene" (excerpt) by Tamara Warren, Free Press special writer. Excerpt reprinted by permission of the *Detroit Free Press*.

Cover: Chubby Checker and the Twist–© Bettmann/CORBIS/BE024930, Background–Shutterstock

Library and Archives Canada Cataloguing in Publication

Swartz, Larry
    The 10 coolest dance crazes / Larry Swartz, Indrani Margolin.

Includes index.
ISBN 978-1-55448-523-9

    1. Readers (Elementary). 2. Readers—Dance. I. Margolin,
Indrani II. Title. III. Title: Ten coolest dance crazes.

PE1117.S9643 2007a   428.6   C2007-906685-2

1 2 3 4 5 6 7 8 9 10   10   17 16 15 14 13 12 11 10 09 08
Printed in Singapore

Contents

Introduction: Bust a Move! 4

Moonwalk 6
Move over NASA — make way for Michael Jackson and his moonwalk.

Vogue 10
Strike a pose! Everyone could be a supermodel with this hot dance craze.

Animal Dances 14
People imitating animals on the dance floor! It might sound strange, but these dances were hot.

Robot 18
In an age of machines and technology, you can't go wrong with dancing the robot!

Electric Slide 22
Whether you are on a cruise, at a wedding, or at a school dance, chances are you'll be doing this dance!

Macarena 26
From the Americas to Europe and Asia — this dance craze swept the world like wildfire.

Hustle 30
Van McCoy's call to the world to "do the hustle" was met with a huge response.

Charleston 34
This might seem like a boring dance, but back in the day, people thought it was wild!

Lindy Hop 38
Jumps, spins, turns, and throws … no wonder the lindy hop is one of the coolest dance crazes of all time.

Twist 42
You don't have to be a pro to do this dance. Just shake and twist your hips to the music!

We Thought … 46

What Do You Think? 47

Index 48

BUST A MOVE!

Has this ever happened to you? You're at a party. You have a belly full of food when you hear the sound of a familiar tune. Suddenly, your friends are rushing to the dance floor. The next moment, their arms are waving and they're jumping and clapping. No, they haven't lost it! They're doing the Macarena.

Dance crazes are often referred to as fad dances. They are specific dances within different styles of dance that become hugely popular for a period of time. Although the style of dance may stick around (for example, break dancing), the dance craze (for example, the moonwalk) fades away. Like most fads, dance crazes are usually associated with a specific time period. They can include solo dances, partner dances, or group dances. But what turns a dance into a craze? Is it the dance or the song? Is it the challenge or the ease of the steps?

In choosing the 10 coolest dance crazes, we considered the following: How long did the craze last? How widespread was the craze? What impact did the craze have on music, other dance styles, and fashion?

So before you jump on the dance floor yelling, "Hey, Macarena!" ask yourself ...

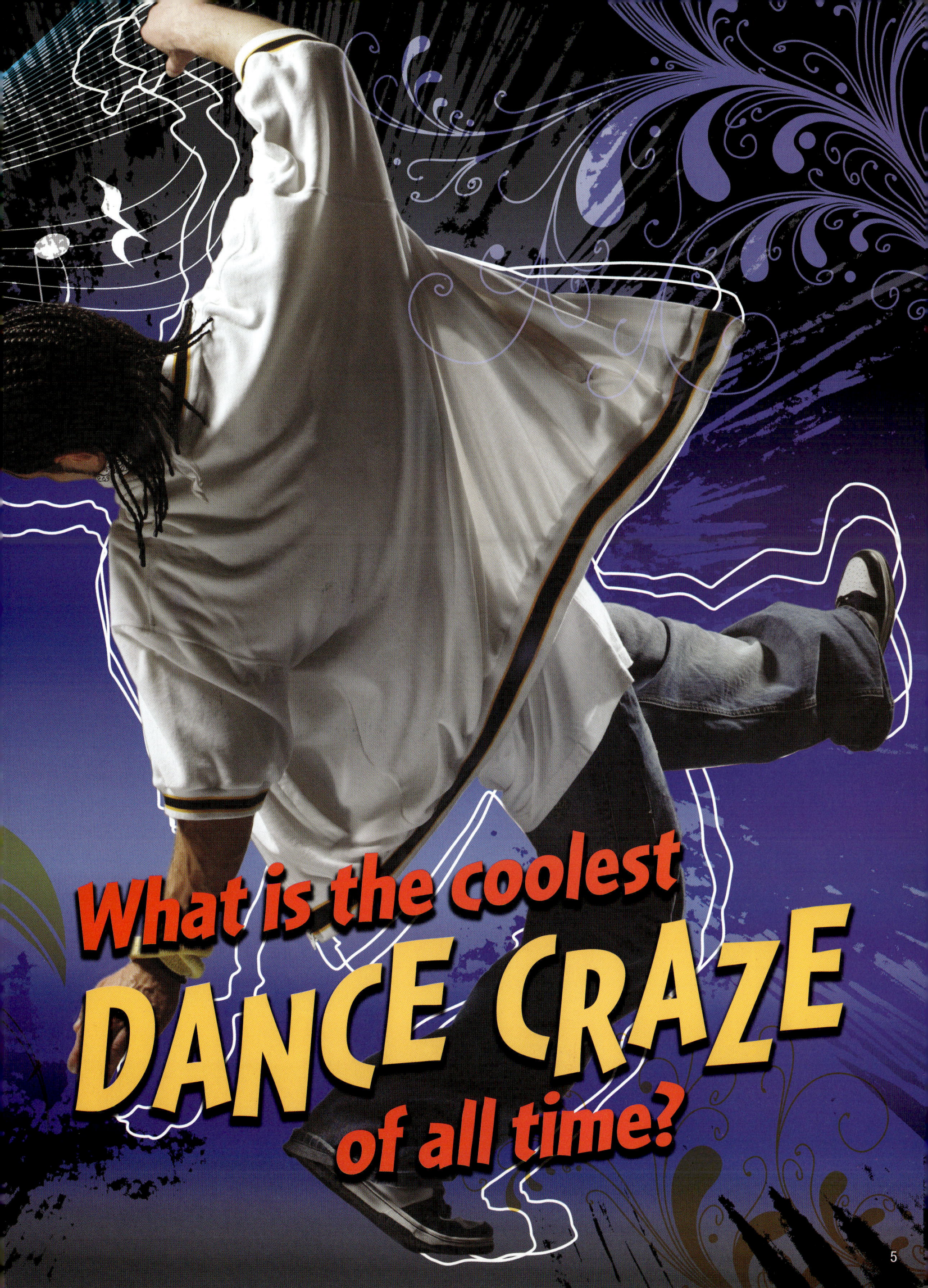

10 MOONWALK

Michael Jackson, seen here onstage in 1984, popularized the moonwalk.

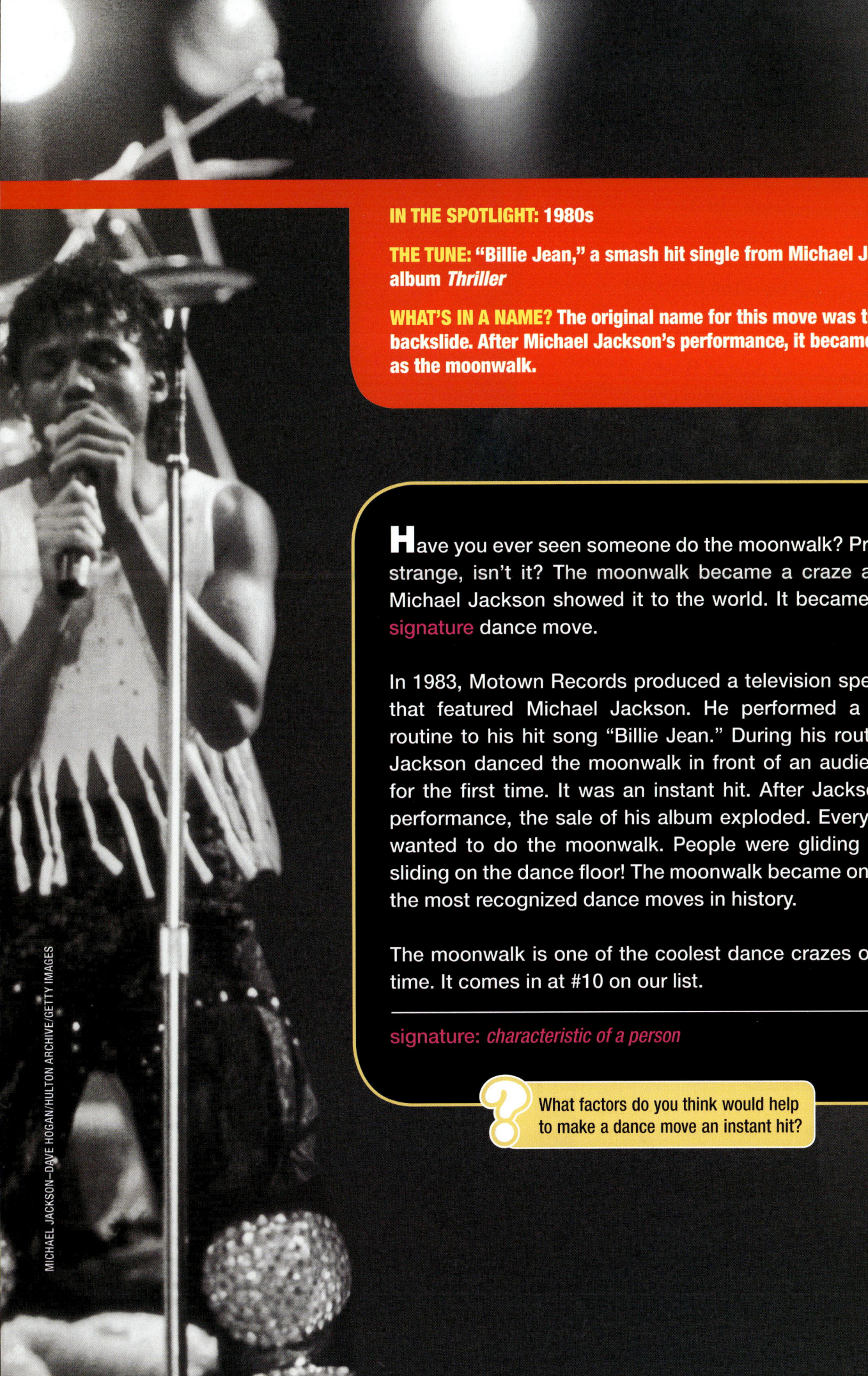

IN THE SPOTLIGHT: 1980s

THE TUNE: "Billie Jean," a smash hit single from Michael Jackson's album *Thriller*

WHAT'S IN A NAME? The original name for this move was the backslide. After Michael Jackson's performance, it became known as the moonwalk.

Have you ever seen someone do the moonwalk? Pretty strange, isn't it? The moonwalk became a craze after Michael Jackson showed it to the world. It became his signature dance move.

In 1983, Motown Records produced a television special that featured Michael Jackson. He performed a live routine to his hit song "Billie Jean." During his routine, Jackson danced the moonwalk in front of an audience for the first time. It was an instant hit. After Jackson's performance, the sale of his album exploded. Everyone wanted to do the moonwalk. People were gliding and sliding on the dance floor! The moonwalk became one of the most recognized dance moves in history.

The moonwalk is one of the coolest dance crazes of all time. It comes in at #10 on our list.

signature: *characteristic of a person*

? What factors do you think would help to make a dance move an instant hit?

MOONWALK

FIRST STEPS

Many people credit Michael Jackson with inventing the moonwalk. In fact, a dance move similar to the moonwalk existed before Jackson's performance. It was known as the backslide, and it was based on a popular mime move. *Solid Gold* dancer Cooley Jackson is often credited with teaching Michael Jackson the moonwalk. Artist James Brown, as well as others, had previously performed versions of the backslide. It was not until Jackson's performance that the move became known as the moonwalk.

mime: *art of telling a story through body movements*

 Do you think it is fair that Michael Jackson gets all of the fame and fortune for the moonwalk?

FANCY FOOTWORK

The purpose of the moonwalk is to give the illusion that you are walking forward, while actually moving backward. It involves floating, gliding, and sliding, which are all popping moves. The instructions for the moonwalk are simple: leave one foot in place and drag the other foot back, lifting up the heel. Repeat with the other foot while walking backward.

popping: *form of dance, which often appears mime-like*

Quick Fact
Michael Jackson's *Thriller* is one of the best-selling albums of all time. It sold more than 50 million copies and made Michael Jackson a huge international success.

Michael Jackson performing onstage at his first solo concert in Kansas City, Missouri, in 1988

LASTING IMPRESSION

Michael Jackson is considered by many to be one of the greatest performers of all time. Although the moonwalk is not an easy move to master, it has attracted the attention of artists and dancers. It has since been adapted into different moves and found its way into other popular dances.

 What are some other dances that seem to have been inspired by the moonwalk?

The Expert Says...
" It's the combinations that really distinguish [Michael] as an artist. Spin, stop, pull up leg, pull jacket open, turn, freeze. And the glide, where he steps forward while pushing back. "

— Hinton Battle, dancer

Master the Moonwalk

It might look like a tough dance, but the moonwalk can be mastered with some practice. All you need are the right shoes, a smooth surface, and a bit of rhythm. Follow these instructions and try it out.

Quick Fact
On January 11, 2006, a man in Ontario, Canada, moonwalked for more than 30 miles. It took him 24 hours!

1. **WEAR THE RIGHT SHOES.** You need soles that are smooth and do not have a lot of grooves.

2. **FIND A FLAT SURFACE TO DANCE ON.** It will allow you to glide more smoothly.

3. **LIFT UP YOUR RIGHT LEG.** Place your toes to the ground about a foot behind your left leg. Increase the width between your legs.

4. **SLIDE YOUR LEFT HEEL BACK** as you lean back on your right leg. Keep your right heel in the air with your toes on the floor.

5. **LIFT YOUR LEFT HEEL OFF THE FLOOR.** At the same time, put the heel of your right foot down.

6. **REPEAT THE LAST TWO STEPS**, going back and forth between your two feet.

TIPS:
- Never let the tips of your feet come off the ground.
- Check yourself out in a mirror to see how you are doing.
- Once you get really good, try doing the moonwalk in one spot.

Take Note
The moonwalk kicks off our list at #10. It introduced a new style of dance to the world and made Michael Jackson a dance sensation. Although the craze itself was short-lived, it got everyone talking. The influence of the moonwalk can be seen in other dances today.
- Do you think the moonwalk deserved all the attention it received? Why or why not?

9 VOGUE

Madonna performing at New York's Madison Square Garden in 2004

IN THE SPOTLIGHT: 1990s

THE TUNE: Madonna's "Vogue" from her album *I'm Breathless*

WHAT'S IN A NAME? The dance was named after the fashion magazine *Vogue* because of its model-like poses.

Can you strike a pose? Then you can vogue! In the words of Madonna, "all you need is your own imagination." Her single, "Vogue," was a huge hit in 1990. It popularized vogue dancing. Dance floors became catwalks. Dancers around the world were strutting around like high-fashion models.

Vogue began in the neighborhoods of New York City. The dance craze sparked by Madonna's song was a simpler version than the one that already existed. Traditional vogue dancers combine elements of jazz, ballet, and even gymnastics. Sometimes it can even look a bit like yoga!

Vogue was one of the most unusual dance crazes the world had ever seen.

catwalks: *narrow, raised walkways used by models in fashion shows*

Why do you think it is easier for a celebrity to introduce a dance craze?

VOGUE

FIRST STEPS

An early form of vogue became popular in Harlem ballrooms in the 1960s. It was called "performance." Social clubs became known as "houses" and they hosted balls where everyone would vogue. Dancers took their moves to more popular clubs and the dance style spread on a small scale. It was not until Madonna released her single that the dance became a hit.

? Why is vogue a good dance for people of all abilities?

FANCY FOOTWORK

When it comes to vogue, almost anything goes. It is a freestyle dance with no set moves. But there are two distinct styles of vogue. The old way (pre-1990) involves quick poses and arm movements. The new way (post-1990) has more rigid movements. Vogue often looks similar to mime.

freestyle: *dance movements with no fixed structure*

Quick Fact
Vogue dancers often have "posing battles" in dance clubs. Dancers are not allowed to touch one another. The dancer with the best poses is the winner.

LASTING IMPRESSION

When Madonna brought vogue into the spotlight, people really got into it. Vogue began showing up in music videos, fashion shows, and movies. Choreographers were putting vogue poses and movements into dance routines. It was the perfect dance for people of all ages and abilities. Although vogue did not survive as a dance craze, there are many people who still enjoy it.

Choreographers: *people who create dances and dance moves*

In vogue, dancers make different shapes and poses with their bodies.

The Expert Says...

"I see a lot of choreographers who could be influenced [by the vogue craze]. I see a big crossover there for stage, for TV, [and] for film."

— David Bronstein, video producer, New York City

STRIKE A POSE

Look at that box dip! What a hairpin! Sound a bit strange to you? Check out this **GLOSSARY** to get familiar with some vogue vocabulary …

ARMS CONTROL: a dancer's "sleight-of-hand" arm and wrist movements

BATTLE: when one vogue dancer challenges another

BOX DIP: a floor pose that involves the legs over the head, with feet planted on the floor in front

CLICKING: a move that involves the arms up over the head and down behind one's back, keeping the hands locked together

DIP: a ground-level stunt

DUCK-WALK: a crouching and foot-sliding movement, which requires balancing on the balls of the feet

HAIRPIN: an extreme backbend dip

LOCKING: freezing from a fast movement and landing in a certain pose

MAKEVELLI: the name of a dip that requires falling to the floor, landing on the back, and using one leg as a lever

POPPING: contracting and relaxing the muscles to cause a jerk in the dancer's body

PYRAMID: several vogue dancers performing together, one in front of the other

SCORPION: a dip inspired by martial arts, with one leg dangling over the head

Quick Fact
Many dance historians argue that break dancing and vogue are close relatives. These dances borrow from each other.

? Can you see yourself doing any of the moves in this glossary? Why or why not?

Take Note
Vogue is #9 on our list. It allowed dancers to be creative on the dance floor by making up their own moves. Vogue is higher on our list than the moonwalk because it can be done by anyone, regardless of his or her dance background. According to Madonna, it doesn't matter if you are a boy or a girl — we can all be superstars on the dance floor!
- Do you think vogue is more of a performance art than a social dance? Explain.

8 ANIMAL DANC[E]

Doris Day performs a barnyard routine in the film By the Light of the Silvery Moon in 1953. During the number she dances the grizzly bear, the chicken reel, the Castle walk, and the turkey trot.

IN THE SPOTLIGHT: 1910s

THE TUNE: Ragtime music

WHAT'S IN A NAME? The dances were called "animal dances" because their moves resembled the moves of animals.

Can turkeys trot? Do bunnies hug? Have you ever seen a kangaroo dip? Where did these dances get their names? In the early 1900s, dancing became much less formal. People danced in restaurants, dance clubs, and even rooftop gardens.

Before animal dances came along, dance was a social ritual. Dances were very formal and lacked the excitement of dance as we know it. Partners held each other at arm's length and followed a controlled pattern of steps.

Animal dances were unlike anything the world had ever seen. There were many people who thought these dances were too wild and crazy. They even outlawed certain steps! That didn't stop the dances from becoming extremely popular. Couples held each other cheek to cheek. Dance moves changed from graceful glides to energetic jogs. Animal dances became one of the coolest dance crazes of all time.

ritual: *set of actions performed for symbolic value*
outlawed: *made illegal*

? Do you think this is a fair criticism? Why or why not?

15

ANIMAL DANCES

FIRST STEPS

At the beginning of the 1900s, the world was changing rapidly. Technology in factories, farms, and in homes cut down on physical labor. This allowed more time for people to socialize. Ragtime music really shook up ballrooms. It featured a steady beat that most likely originated from the military march. Along with its "ragged" melodies, ragtime was a unique sound that was perfect for dancing! The existing dance moves no longer fit the music. Most animal dances were born in African American communities. Dancers stomped, wiggled, and expressed themselves in unique ways.

FANCY FOOTWORK

There were many different kinds of animal dances. Some of the most popular included the bunny hug, turkey trot, and grizzly bear. Most dances involved slouching, shoulders shaking, and tight embracing. Dancers pumped their arms and wiggled their bottoms like never before. Most dances did not have a set number of steps, so people could make up moves as they danced.

Quick Fact
Between 1912 and 1914, when ragtime was popular, more than one hundred new dance steps were created. As music changed, so did the dances that accompanied it.

LASTING IMPRESSION

Until animal dances came along, couples were supposed to keep their excitement under control on the dance floor. Dancing was a social tradition, rather than something to be done for enjoyment. Animal dances were simple and fun. Although most animal dances did not stick around very long, they changed the way people thought about dance. One of the animal dances, the fox trot, is still performed today. It has evolved into a smoother, more graceful dance.

Quick Fact
The fox trot was created by actor Harry Fox on the roof of the New York Theatre. Vernon and Irene Castle, two famous ragtime dancers, made it popular by slowing it down and giving it a more graceful look.

Vernon and Irene Castle

Dance Like an Animal

There's the grizzly bear, the bunny hug, the camel walk, and many more! Read these profiles to learn more about these wacky dances.

Grizzly Bear

The grizzly bear was a rough dance that resembled the actions of — you guessed it — a grizzly bear. It began in San Francisco. Dancers held each other close while moving forward with heavy steps. It also included off-balance sways and bent-knee dips.

Fox Trot

The fox trot is one of the only animal dances that is still performed today. Its original moves have been adapted to suit newer dances, such as swing or ballroom. It combines both slow and quick steps and can be done on the spot or moving around the room.

Bunny Hug

There was a whole lot of shaking going on in this dance! Dancers would shake and wiggle their bodies to the music. Couples were often kicked out of clubs for dancing this one.

Turkey Trot

This animal dance was one of the first ones to catch on. It involved a springy walk with feet well apart and swinging up-and-down shoulders. It was not a graceful dance. There were people who were so upset about this dance that they tried to have it banned.

> **?** Why do you think people would have been angry about this dance?

Camel Walk

The camel walk was similar to the famous fox trot. Dancers stood straight up, moved in a zigzag direction, and dragged their steps. The camel walk came back in the 1950s, but it no longer involved a partner.

Quick Fact

In 1912, 15 women from Pennsylvania were fired from their jobs for dancing the turkey trot on their lunch break!

The Expert Says…

"By 1910, the popular phrase was 'Everybody's Doin' It Now,' but in fact most of middle and upper class society was only talking about it. They could not yet accept the new ragtime dances …"

— Richard Powers, dance historian, Stanford University

Take Note

Animal dances stomp into the #8 spot. These unique dances really stirred things up in the world of social dancing. People were moving around the dance floor in ways they had never moved before. Although vogue was a big hit, animal dances helped set the stage for future social dances.
- Compare this dance to the moonwalk or vogue. What do you like or dislike about each dance craze? Why?

5   4   3   2   1

7 ROBOT

The robot is best danced to music known as "electrofunk." The distinct beat of the music makes the moves more dramatic.

IN THE SPOTLIGHT: 1970s and 1980s

THE TUNE: The Jackson 5's "Dancing Machine" and anything with a funky beat!

WHAT'S IN A NAME? The robot or robot dancing involves moving your body like a robot or mannequin.

You have probably seen someone dance the robot at some point in your life. It might have been a joke, or even an honest attempt, but one thing is for certain … it's hard to take this dance seriously. When Michael Jackson first performed it on the TV program *Soul Train*, people were blown away. He looked just like a machine!

The robot existed before Michael Jackson performed it on television. It was a popular move for street mimes, but it was Jackson's performance that brought the dance to millions of viewers. It was not long before people became hooked. The dance became a phenomenon. Dance floors everywhere were filled with people trying to copy Jackson's mechanical moves.

The robot was a short-lived dance craze, but it never disappeared completely. It has managed to creep up in dances from time to time. In the late 1990s, break dancing was more popular than ever, and the robot was reborn.

Check out why we feel the robot deserves to be on a list of the coolest dance crazes …

? Why do you think a dance might disappear and become popular again years later?

ROBOT DANCER–MICHAEL OCHS ARCHIVES/CORBIS

ROBOT

FIRST STEPS

Many people credit dancer Robert Shields with creating this dance. In 1967, Shields worked as a human mannequin and danced like a robot as part of his act. Eventually he became a mime and brought his moves to the streets of San Francisco. Shields's dance moves were quickly adopted by street dancers who were always looking for new moves. Michael Jackson introduced the move to the world on *Soul Train* and the rest is history.

 **Why do you think street dances often become dance crazes?**

FANCY FOOTWORK

You don't need fancy feet for this one. This dance is all about the arms. Start with a very stiff posture. Then move your body parts at the joints, starting and stopping as though they are connected to hinges. The key is to look as robotic as possible. The broken robot is another version of the robot dance. It is similar to the robot, but it resembles a robot in distress!

LASTING IMPRESSION

In the late 1980s, the robot disappeared as quickly as it came. But it wasn't gone for good! The dance became an important part of break dancing culture, and it has inspired a whole new group of "robotic" movements. Robot dancing has popped up everywhere in popular culture. From soccer players to SpongeBob SquarePants, people can't seem to get enough of this dance. The robot is clearly here to stay!

Quick Fact
The robot dance is so popular, even Homer and Marge Simpson danced it at a wedding in an episode of *The Simpsons*.

The Expert Says...
> I was getting bored standing like a statue. I started developing isolated movements, and the robot was born. ... You're watching a human body animate itself. People can't keep their eyes off it.

— Robert Shields, dancer

In 2006, Peter Crouch, an English soccer player, danced the robot to celebrate a goal. It became such a famous moment that Prince William asked him to do it again at a practice he attended.

10   9   8   7   6

BREAK IT!

The robot was only one of many break dancing moves to make it big. Check out this list of some other popular moves that are still kicking around break dancing circles today …

TOPROCK
These are steps that allow dancers to warm up for more acrobatic moves.

DOWNROCK
All footwork performed on the floor is known as downrock. It allows a dancer to show off foot speed and control.

FREEZES
Freezes are when all motion freezes and the dancer stays in a "frozen" pose.

POWER MOVES
These are the most impressive part of a breaker's routine. Dancers who use too many are known as "power heads."

WINDMILL
This is a move where dancers spin from their upper backs to their chests while twirling their legs around in a V-shape.

HANDSPINS
Dancers perform this move by spinning themselves by their hands!

HEADSPINS
Exactly as it sounds — dancers spin while balancing on their heads!

Take Note

Although it was short-lived as a craze, the robot has managed to survive on dance floors, in TV shows, and even in commercials. For surviving the test of time and sticking around for a longer period of time than animal dances, the robot wins the #7 spot on our list.

- The robot has become a popular break dancing move. Research break dancing to find out how it has changed over the years.

6 ELECTRIC SLI

The electric slide is the perfect party dance. It can be danced alone or with a group of people.

DE

IN THE SPOTLIGHT: Late 1980s and 1990s

THE TUNE: "Electric Boogie," by Marcia Griffiths and written by Bunny Wailer

WHAT'S IN A NAME? The dance was originally called the electric. It came from the first line in the song "Electric Boogie." People started calling it the electric slide after a different line in the song.

If you like to dance in a big group, the electric slide is the dance for you. Not only is it fun, it's electric! If you have ever been to a wedding or other celebration and saw people lining up to grapevine across the dance floor, they were probably dancing the electric slide. The electric slide is popular in social dancing. It allows people to get down on the dance floor as a group.

Whether you are on a cruise in the Caribbean or at a wedding in the United States, chances are the electric slide will be there. Although the electric slide was more popular in the early 1990s than it is today, it has survived the test of time.

The electric slide slips into the #6 spot on our list.

grapevine: *dance step that includes a series of side steps and one leg crossing over the other*

 What features do you think a dance must have in order to "survive the test of time"?

ELECTRIC SLIDE

FIRST STEPS

In 1976, the electric slide was created by dancer Ric Silver. It was performed for the re-opening of a disco named "Vamps" in New York City. The dance was originally more difficult, but it was simplified for less experienced dancers. It wasn't until Marcia Griffith's song "Electric Boogie" was re-released in 1989 that the electric slide became an international craze. As the song gained popularity, so did the dance.

FANCY FOOTWORK

The electric slide is a basic four-wall line dance. This means a dancer will directly face four different walls while performing the dance. It includes a total of 22 steps. The dance was created in numeric order. It has three 3-steps, two 2-steps, one 1-step, and a hop. It can be danced in a single line, double line, or with lines weaving in and out of each another.

Quick Fact

Ric Silver created the electric slide with 22 steps because his birthday is on January 22nd. While the basic electric slide is an easy dance, a more advanced dancer can introduce new moves and make it more challenging.

LASTING IMPRESSION

Although the popularity of the electric slide peaked in the early 1990s, it is still danced on many social occasions. When it came out, the electric slide sparked a huge interest in line dancing. It was soon followed by other popular line dances, such as dances to Billy Ray Cyrus's famous "Achy Breaky Heart." Dance crazes today, such as the cha cha slide, prove that line dancing is just as popular as ever.

> **The Expert Says...**
> "I have a very unique style to my dance. A flow that is easily picked up. Most of my students through the years have always found my choreography easy to 'put on.'"
> — Ric Silver, dancer and choreographer of the electric slide

The electric slide is for everyone — people of all ages can join in the fun.

The Fight for the Electric Slide

Who would have thought a dance could cause so many problems? Check out this **article** about Ric Silver's fight to keep the electric slide in its original form.

When choreographer Ric Silver saw online videos of people dancing the electric slide, he was not happy. The dance he had created back in 1976 had changed. There was even video of someone dancing it (incorrectly) on stilts! When it was performed incorrectly on *The Oprah Winfrey Show* and *The Ellen DeGeneres Show*, Silver decided to put the copyright he had received in 2004 to use.

Ric Silver contacted those who, he felt, had violated copyright law. YouTube dancers who had posted videos of the dance were notified. Even major Hollywood companies were getting sued. This made some people angry. They decided to fight back.

? What would you do if you were contacted by Ric Silver? Explain.

On May 22, 2007, Ric Silver and the Electronic Frontier Foundation (EFF) came to an agreement. The dance would hold a Creative Commons license. This meant the dance could be used for **non-commercial** purposes.

In the future, Silver will not be making claims against anyone for dancing the electric slide, unless they are making money from it. So don't worry — the home video of your wild Aunt Suzie doing the electric slide is no problem. If you want to put it in a movie, however, you will have to take it up with Mr. Silver.

non-commercial: *not-for-profit*

Take Note

No wonder the electric slide has become so famous. It's the perfect social dance! It can be danced alone, with a partner, or in a group. It can be modified for beginners, average dancers, and even experts. The electric slide is higher on our list than the robot because it was embraced by a broader dance community. For its worldwide popularity and long life, the electric slide comes in at #6 on our list.

- The creator of the electric slide has copyrighted the dance to ensure that it is done correctly. Do you think that a dance should be copyrighted? Give reasons for your answer.

5 MACARENA

Dancers performing the Macarena at a Coconuts music store October 15, 1996, in New York City

IN THE SPOTLIGHT: 1990s

THE TUNE: "Macarena," by the band Los del Rio

WHAT'S IN A NAME? The dance is named after the song "Macarena." Macarena is the name of the woman in the song.

It was big. It holds the world record for the most people performing one dance at the same time. If you have not already guessed, it's the Macarena. The Macarena first hit California in 1993. It was already huge in Spain, Europe, and Mexico. Suddenly, it was everywhere. It became one of the most popular dance crazes the world had ever seen. Even people in India and the Philippines were doing it!

In the summer of 1996, the hit single "Macarena" was #1 on the *Billboard* Hot 100 for 14 weeks. The dance was a simple line dance with a Cuban flair. The Macarena was in nightclubs, on TV, and in movies. It was even done at a presidential convention in 1996.

The Macarena is one of the biggest dance crazes of recent times. It dances its way into the #5 spot on our list.

? How do you think a dance might spread around the world?

MACARENA

FIRST STEPS
Los del Rio was inspired to write "Macarena" after seeing a flamenco dancer in Venezuela. The song did not originally have a dance. Although little is known about the origin of the dance, one report says Los del Rio made the dance up on stage one night and the audience followed along. Another report credits "Macarena" herself for the dance. Wherever it started, it could not be stopped!

flamenco: *traditional Spanish dance*

FANCY FOOTWORK
You don't have to be a rocket scientist to dance this one! First, arms out in front, palms down. Then turn palms up. Touch your shoulders, hips, and the top of your bum. Each move should be done one arm at a time (right, then left). Arms should touch the opposite side of the body. Swing your hips, jump a quarter turn, and yell, "Hey, Macarena!"

LASTING IMPRESSION
The Macarena was a hit in popular culture. The song and dance showed up in TV commercials, video games, movies, and cartoons. A computer screen saver called "Hey, Macaroni" came out, which showed pieces of elbow macaroni doing the dance. It was the biggest hit dance on cruises and at school dances. Even today, dancers young and old rush to the dance floor with the first beat of the song.

? Can you think of a reason that the Macarena was a bigger part of popular culture than other dances on our list?

Los del Rio performing at Coconuts music store

Quick Fact
The Macarena was so famous, and spread so quickly, that a computer virus was named after it!

The Expert Says...
"Dance crazes like the Macarena allow us to 'break' our normal rules about dance. One way they allow this is by being very simple (as the Macarena was), or by teaching the dance at each occasion (as the Macarena often was). I think we like breaking the rules and letting everybody in on the fun sometimes."

— Melinda Russell, associate professor of music, Carleton University

U.S. HEARS THE BEAT OF MACARENA DANCE CRAZE

By Kathleen Barnes

When the Macarena caught on in the 1990s, it spread like a virus. Go back in time with this article from April 1996 and find out how the craze took the world by surprise …

(CNN) — The thumping Spanish beat just makes your feet want to dance. Your hips swing, and your body shakes all over. The Macarena, recorded by Spanish flamenco artists Los del Rio two years ago, has suddenly caught fire.

? What features might a dance have that make it appealing to large groups of people?

It set a record recently in Britain by jumping 63 places on the pop music singles chart into the top 10, and is a chart-topping hit in virtually every European country.

The new dance craze has made its way to Beirut, Bosnia, and Brisbane. And it's leaped to the United States, where 50,000 hip-swinging baseball fans wiggled their way to a world line-dancing record at Yankee Stadium.

Rafael Ruiz and Romero Monge of Los del Rio are quick to point out that they aren't new — they've been making music for more than 30 years. …

These days, you just have to Macarena to be anybody.

Instructions for the hand-jiving dance have even been published in newspapers, but it doesn't matter if you haven't got it quite right — the beat will take you there.

hand-jiving: type of dance involving a pattern of clapping, thigh slapping, and other hand movements

Quick Fact
Al Gore danced the Macarena during his 1996 speech at the Democratic National Convention.

Take Note
The Macarena ranks #5 on our list of the coolest dance crazes because of its worldwide popularity. It is a simple dance that people of all ages can do. A party wasn't a party without the Macarena! Due to its huge impact on popular culture, the Macarena comes in higher on our list than the electric slide.
- Have you ever danced the Macarena? Why do you think this dance has been so popular?

5 4 3 2 1

4 HUSTLE

Saturday Night Fever, *the musical, at the Apollo Victoria Theatre in London in 2004*

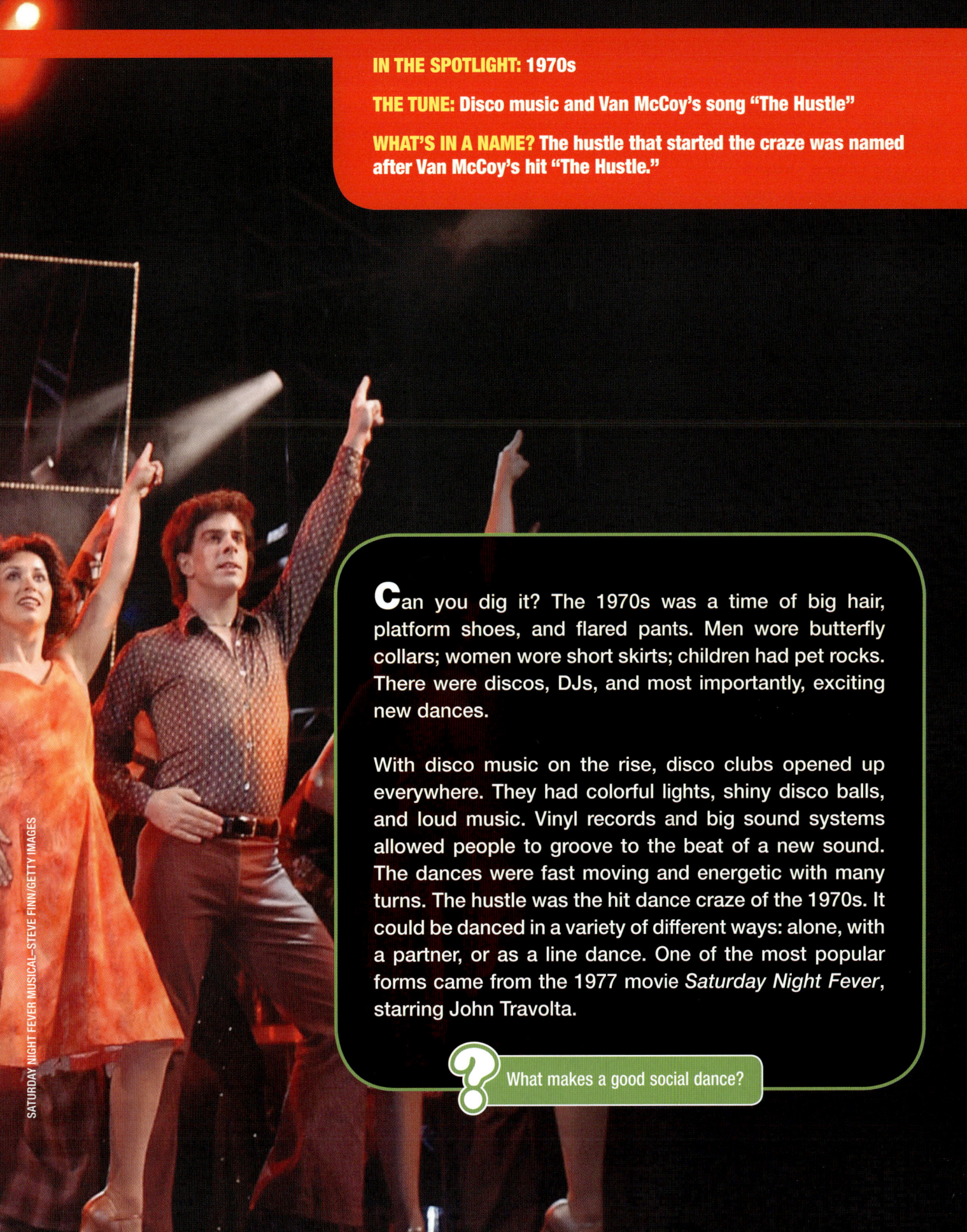

IN THE SPOTLIGHT: 1970s

THE TUNE: Disco music and Van McCoy's song "The Hustle"

WHAT'S IN A NAME? The hustle that started the craze was named after Van McCoy's hit "The Hustle."

Can you dig it? The 1970s was a time of big hair, platform shoes, and flared pants. Men wore butterfly collars; women wore short skirts; children had pet rocks. There were discos, DJs, and most importantly, exciting new dances.

With disco music on the rise, disco clubs opened up everywhere. They had colorful lights, shiny disco balls, and loud music. Vinyl records and big sound systems allowed people to groove to the beat of a new sound. The dances were fast moving and energetic with many turns. The hustle was the hit dance craze of the 1970s. It could be danced in a variety of different ways: alone, with a partner, or as a line dance. One of the most popular forms came from the 1977 movie *Saturday Night Fever*, starring John Travolta.

? What makes a good social dance?

HUSTLE

FIRST STEPS

The Latin-inspired hustle was born in the clubs of New York City in the 1970s. It was the return of closed-couple dancing, in which the dancers put their arms around each other. Although it is often thought of as a simple partner dance, the hustle exists in many different forms. It can include quick steps, slow steps, line dancing, and even elements of swing. When Van McCoy recorded "The Hustle" in 1975, the hustle became a huge hit.

The Expert Says...

" A whole new field of entertainment was introduced. … These opportunities fueled the fire, and the young dancers continued to seek out new ways to excite the club audiences. The [hustle] became faster and more exciting … "

— Billy Fajardo, professional dancer and choreographer

FANCY FOOTWORK

Do the hustle! There's only one problem — choosing which hustle to do. The hustle refers to a few different dances. Generally, all forms of the hustle borrow from swing and Latin dancing and include lots of spins. Dancers can do the hustle with a partner, which is more like a ballroom dance. It can include wraps, twirls, and lifts. The hustle is also a popular line dance.

LASTING IMPRESSION

Disco dancing began a whole new world of nightlife. By the end of the 1970s, the U.S. had more than 15,000 discos. People everywhere left the comfort of their couches to try out John Travolta's famous moves. Disco dancing brought couples back together on the dance floor and convinced people that dancing was cool. Disco dancing and the hustle changed the way people dressed, socialized, and most importantly, "grooved."

? Why do you think dances can influence the way people dress?

John Travolta dancing in Saturday Night Fever

Quick Fact
Saturday Night Fever is credited with making disco popular. Travolta showed men and women a new way to move on the dance floor.

The hustle is still hot on Detroit dance scene

The hustle was hot back in the day, and it's still hot today! Read this article from the *Detroit Free Press* to find out why the hustle is still steaming up the dance floor ...

Detroit Free Press, May 31, 2007
By Tamara Warren

DETROIT — Hundreds of women and a handful of men line up on the dance floor in neat rows every Thursday night at Rhythm Universe on Detroit's west side, waiting for the cue from hustle instructor Alyce Razor-Bey. "Step to the right. Step to the left. Ballroom turn. Cha-cha. Kick, turn. Now roll."

On the Detroit hustle scene, these are familiar commands — the play-by-play instructions that make up the steps in the stylized line dance that's been taking dance parties by storm.

The line dance, widely associated with the disco scene of the 1970s and the 1975 No. 1 hit "The Hustle" by Van McCoy and the Soul City Symphony, has seen a resurgence over the past decade, and especially during the past few years. ...

Though there are pockets of hustle activity all over the United States, the surging popularity of the dance is particularly keen in metro Detroit. ...

When Detroiters hit the dance floor to do some hustling, they're not moving their feet to the Van McCoy tune, but instead to a nearly endless number of songs and remixes that work rhythmically for the many variations of the line dance. Detroit hustles draw from other dances popular in the area, including ballroom, cha-cha, and step-dancing. ...

resurgence: *revival; growth in popularity*

Quick Fact
The hustle comes in all shapes and sizes! The modern couple hustle is sometimes called the New York hustle. There was also the basic hustle, the swing hustle, and even the sling hustle. And that's not all of them!

Take Note
Although the Macarena was a big hit, the hustle developed into dozens of dances, which are still popular today. It allows people to dance solo, in a group, or in the arms of a partner. The hustle has danced its way to the #4 spot on our list.
- Go online to research two different ways of dancing the hustle. Which one would you prefer to dance, and why?

3 CHARLESTON

The Charleston was often danced by flappers — the modern women of the 1920s.

IN THE SPOTLIGHT: 1920s

THE TUNE: "The Charleston," by James P. Johnson, from the Broadway musical *Runnin' Wild*

WHAT'S IN A NAME? This dance was named after the town Charleston, in South Carolina.

If you have ever seen the Charleston, you probably thought it looked like an old-fashioned dance that could put you to sleep. Believe it or not, people once thought this dance was wild and crazy!

The Charleston was one of the biggest dance crazes of the 1920s. It started off in African American communities and moved to white neighborhoods across the United States. Although dancing had relaxed since the waltz and other ballroom dances were introduced, people were uncomfortable with the kicks, swings, and high-energy moves of the Charleston. It was banned in some towns and on some college campuses. But this seemed only to make the dance more popular! At this time, women "bobbed" their hair like boys, hiked up their skirts, and pulled up their sleeves. The free-spirited Charleston was the perfect dance for them!

The Charleston was a dance that reflected the changing times. Check out how this dance craze influenced music and fashion for future generations.

? Can you think of a modern-day dance that is considered wild? Explain.

CHARLESTON

The Charleston

FIRST STEPS
Dance scholars have a few different theories about how the Charleston began. Many credit the dockworkers of Charleston, South Carolina, with creating the steps that would eventually become the Charleston. It was not until the musical *Runnin' Wild* in 1923 that the dance became an international craze. People danced the Charleston for hours at dance marathons.

FANCY FOOTWORK
Get ready for some fancy footwork! The Charleston can be danced alone, with a partner, or in a group. The basic Charleston involves stepping back with the right foot and kicking back with the left, then stepping forward with the left foot and kicking forward with the right. Arms are swung side to side in the opposite direction of the feet. The most popular move includes crossing the hands back and forth on the knees as they open and close.

LASTING IMPRESSION
The Charleston was danced by people of different backgrounds and experiences. It was much less rigid than earlier dances and showed people's desire to let loose in a more relaxed environment. Women could dance on their own, without a partner. The Charleston led the way for other popular dances such as the lindy hop.

> **The Expert Says...**
>
> "The Charleston was the first African American dance to be almost universally popular in the U.S. This was due in part to several new inventions: the radio, the phonograph, and the silent film."
>
> — Bob E. Thomas, performer

? Now that you know the moves, why do you think some people were bothered by the Charleston?

Quick Fact
Dance marathons could go on for hundreds of hours. After the death of a few dancers, these marathons were outlawed in many states.

Dance marathons were popular in the 1920s. The Charleston was often performed at these marathons.

DANGEROUS Dancing

When the Charleston first came out, people were outraged. It was "crazier" than any dance they had seen before. So what came before the Charleston? Find out in this timeline of "wild" social dances ...

1740 — The **QUADRILLE** is a dance usually performed by four couples in a square formation. It was first introduced in France.

1780s — Polite society was appalled when the **WALTZ** became popular in Austria and Germany. It was the first time men and women danced together closely instead of at arm's length.

1830s — The **CANCAN** featured a line of high-kicking women. As this dance became wilder and more energetic, it was seen by many to be immoral.

1890s — The **CAKEWALK** first appeared on sugarcane plantations. This dance craze broke the tradition of smooth gliding dance steps that had been popular in the past.

1910 — **ANIMAL DANCES** really shook things up (see #8 on our list). People spent time in jail for performing these dances.

1923 — The **CHARLESTON** was considered to be such a wild dance that some places put up signs like "PCQ," meaning Please Charleston Quietly.

immoral: *against the beliefs of a time; wrong*

The Quadrille

The Cancan

Take Note

The Charleston kicks its way into the #3 spot. In the 1920s, it was an international dance craze. It not only introduced a brand new way of moving — flapping the arms and kicking the legs — but it influenced the way people dressed and acted. It was easy to learn and allowed people to dance with or without a partner.

• Compare and contrast at least two dances from the 1920s with today's popular dances.

5 4 **3** 2 1

2 LINDY HOP

The lindy hop includes both solo and partner dancing.

IN THE SPOTLIGHT: 1930s

THE TUNE: Jazz music (swing)

WHAT'S IN A NAME? The lindy hop was named after Charles Lindbergh's famous transatlantic flight. In the late 1930s, the lindy hop was often referred to as the jitterbug. The term jitterbug is often used to describe all kinds of swing dancing.

It's time for a breakaway! No, we're not talking about hockey. It's the lindy hop. If you have ever seen people gather around a great dancer on the dance floor, you have seen a breakaway. Believe it or not, these "jam circles," or "breakaways," come from the time of the lindy hop. Dancers would step aside and circle around lindy hoppers who could really put on a show.

The lindy hop came out of the Charleston and a few other popular social dances. It includes wild acrobatics and fancy footwork. Frankie "Musclehead" Manning created the first lindy air step in 1935. The dance became more popular than ever. People everywhere flocked to the Savoy Ballroom in New York City. It was the famous home of the lindy hop.

Check out why the lindy hop deserves the #2 spot on our list of the coolest dance crazes …

? How do you think a dance develops? Explain.

LINDY HOP

Quick Fact

Some popular moves included swingouts, sugar pushes, and the Shorty George, named after dancer George Snowden. He was one of the top dancers in the Savoy Ballroom.

FIRST STEPS

The lindy hop began in the 1920s and 1930s in Harlem, New York. It borrowed some moves from earlier dance crazes, such as the Charleston and the fox trot. The energetic sound of the jazz music invited couples to boogie on the dance floor. If you were a lindy hopper, the Savoy Ballroom was the place to be. Its dance floor was more than a block long!

FANCY FOOTWORK

Grab a partner for this one! The lindy hop is full of jumps, spins, turns, and throws. It blends African rhythms with European dance. In the late 1930s, a slower, more relaxed lindy hop was introduced. This made it an easier dance for average dancers. The dance was still full of energy, but it lacked the flips and air steps.

? Why is it important for a dance craze to be easy for the average dancer?

LASTING IMPRESSION

The lindy hop is the granddaddy of all swing dances. It was an exciting new dance that was also fun to watch. It became a big part of popular culture, appearing in movies, theaters, and nightclubs. In 1943, *Life* magazine called swing dancing "America's National Dance."

Performing the lindy hop at the Savoy

The Expert Says...

"Now lindy hop, itself, is done to swing music. And, if you know what a swing is, it's very smooth and it flows, so lindy hop flows along with this music."

— Frankie Manning, dancer and choreographer

LINDY HOP LEGEND

Frankie "Musclehead" Manning was one of the greatest lindy hoppers to grace the Savoy Ballroom. Read this **profile** to find out why he has been called the ambassador of the lindy hop.

In the 1930s, people from all over traveled to the Savoy to share in the great music and dancing. One of these people, Frankie Manning, would never walk out the same. He became one of the leading dancers and choreographers in a group known as Whitey's Lindy Hoppers. The group included some of the most talented dancers of the time. They danced live performances, bringing the lindy hop to people around the world.

Lucille Middleton and Frankie Manning doing a drop-down-the-back move while on tour with Hollywood Hotel Review *in New Zealand, summer 1938*

? Why was this a good way to introduce dances at this time?

Frankie Manning started dancing as a young teenager. He had a unique style and invented many creative moves, including the famous lindy air step. This is where the man sends his partner flying through the air in an over-the-back roll. Manning became famous and danced with lindy hop stars such as Norma Miller. He appeared in Broadway productions and in movies.

Today, Frankie Manning is more than 90 years old, but age hasn't stopped him. He can still be found lindy hopping! Manning works to keep swing dancing alive by serving on the board of directors for the New York Swing Dance Society.

Quick Fact
The Savoy Ballroom was a place where both African Americans and white people could dance. At the time, many places did not allow this.

Take Note
The lindy hop comes in at #2 on our list. Although the Charleston was very popular, the lindy hop introduced a brand new style of dance — swing! Since then, many different forms of swing have developed. Although the lindy hop can be a complicated performance dance, it can also be slowed down and simplified for the average dancer.
- Today the lindy hop is more of a competitive and performance dance than a social dance. Why might a dance lose its appeal?

5   4   3   **2**   1

1 TWIST

Singer Chubby Checker twists with a dance partner in London.

IN THE SPOTLIGHT: 1960s

THE TUNE: "The Twist," written by Hank Ballard and the Midnighters and popularized by singer Chubby Checker

WHAT'S IN A NAME? The twist was named after its moves, which involve twisting the hips from side to side.

In 1960, a song called "The Twist" by singer Chubby Checker invited America to "do the twist" — a new dance that required very little technique. Checker's invitation was met with a huge response and the twist became the ultimate dance craze.

In the 1950s and 1960s, the TV show *American Bandstand* brought music and dance to people around the world. Dance crazes came and went faster than ever. The twist was danced to a hit rock and roll tune. It spread like wildfire within a year. It was fun, and it didn't matter if you didn't have a date. This one could be danced solo! The twist was also popular because it was simple. It could be done by people of all ages, regardless of their dance background.

The twist tops our list of the 10 coolest dance crazes. Read on to find out why …

TWIST

FIRST STEPS
Hank Ballard and the Midnighters was the first band to record the song "The Twist." They twisted their bodies while they performed the song. A form of twisting had already appeared in the lindy hop and other swing dances. In 1960, singer Chubby Checker re-recorded the song and it rose to the top of the charts. Checker showed the world how to dance the twist when he appeared on *American Bandstand* and *The Ed Sullivan Show*.

? Do you think television plays a role in how quickly dance crazes come and go? Why?

FANCY FOOTWORK
You don't have to be a genius to figure this one out! It can be danced alone or with a group. With one foot forward, imagine you are squashing bugs with the balls of your feet. Now imagine you are drying off your back with a towel. Twist your body back and forth. That's all there is to it!

LASTING IMPRESSION
The twist was the first rock and roll dance style where people did not have to touch each other. People danced it in nightclubs, in schoolyards, and in their homes. Dozens of rock and roll songs came out with the word "twist" in them. Hundreds of short-lived dance crazes rocked the nation.

Chubby Checker twists with a friend in 1961.

The Expert Says...
"[T]he style of dancing that was popularized with the twist … has been adopted through the years by generations of young people and their seniors, swaying to the sounds of rock and roll."
— Carol Sears Botsch, associate professor, University of South Carolina Aiken

Quick Fact
People flocked to New York's Peppermint Lounge to dance the twist. The lounge was so popular that another dance craze, the peppermint twist, was named after it.

IT'S ALL IN THE NAME

The twist inspired a series of dance crazes that shared a common feature — the name of the dance appeared in the name of the song. Check out these descriptions of some of the most popular dances that came from rock and roll songs...

THE FREDDY

This dance came out of the song "Do the Freddie" by Freddie and the Dreamers. It involves sticking out your left leg and left arm and then right leg and right arm to the beat of the music. That's all there is to it!

? Why do you think a music artist would want a dance craze to accompany his or her song?

THE MONKEY

This dance was done to Major Lance's hit "The Monkey Time." Dancers waved their hands in the air and bobbed their heads from side to side. They even scratched their armpits like monkeys!

THE MASHED POTATO

This dance was a hit in 1962. It was danced to Dee Dee Sharp's "Mashed Potato Time." This one is similar to the twist, but it looks more like the dancer is mashing potatoes with his or her feet.

THE PONY

This one was another Chubby Checker hit. It was danced to the song "Pony Time." Although it wasn't as famous as Checker's "The Twist," it was still a hit. Dancers moved their feet quickly like a trotting pony.

Quick Fact
In the 1960s, Bill Haley & His Comets recorded a song called "The Spanish Twist." He is often credited with starting the twist dance craze in Latin America.

Take Note
The twist tops our list of coolest dance crazes. It created a dance sensation around the world. The twist inspired dozens of other dance crazes in its day, and it is still popular almost half a century later. It appeals to people of all ages because it is fun and easy to do.
• What is the current dance craze? Who does it appeal to? Why?

We Thought …

Here are the criteria we used in ranking the 10 coolest dance crazes.

The dance:
- Created new styles of dance
- Appealed to people of all age groups
- Changed the way people socialized
- Influenced other dances
- Gained worldwide popularity
- Could be modified for all dance backgrounds
- Survived the test of time
- Allowed people to express themselves
- Influenced popular culture

Index

A

American Bandstand, 43–44
Animal dances, 14–17, 21, 37
Apollo Victoria Theatre, 30

B

Backslide, 7–8
Ballet, 11
Battle, Hinton, 8
Bill Haley & His Comets, 45
Billboard, 27
Billie Jean, 7
Botsch, Carol Sears, 44
Break dancing, 4, 13, 19–21
Bronstein, David, 12
Brown, James, 8
Bunny hug, 16–17

C

Cakewalk, 37
California, 27
Camel walk, 17
Canada, 9
Cancan, 37
Castle, Irene and Vernon, 16
Castle walk, 14
Charleston, 34–37, 39–41
Checker, Chubby, 42–45
Chicken dance, 47
Crouch, Peter, 20
Cyrus, Billy Ray, 24

D

Dancing Machine, 19
Day, Doris, 14
Detroit, 33
Disco, 24, 31–33

E

Ed Sullivan Show, The, 44
Electric Boogie, 23–24
Electric slide, 22–25, 29
Ellen DeGeneres Show, The, 25

F

Fajardo, Billy, 32
Flamenco, 28–29
Flappers, 34
Fox, Harry, 16
Fox trot, 16–17, 40
Freddy, 45
Freestyle, 12

G

Gore, Al, 29
Griffiths, Marcia, 23
Grizzly bear, 14, 16–17
Gymnastics, 11

H

Hank Ballard and the Midnighters, 43–44
Hustle, 30–33

I

India, 27

J

Jackson, Cooley, 8
Jackson, Michael, 6–9, 19–20
Jazz, 11, 39–40
Jitterbug, 39
Johnson, James P., 35

K

Ketchup dance, 47

L

Life, 40
Lindbergh, Charles, 39
Lindy hop, 36, 38–41, 44
Line dancing, 24, 27, 31–33
London, 30, 42
Los Del Rio, 27–29

M

Macarena, 4, 26–29, 33
Madison Square Garden, 10
Madonna, 10–13
Manning, Frankie, 39–41
Marathons, 36
Mashed potato, 45
McCoy, Van, 31–33
Middleton, Lucille, 41
Miller, Norma, 41
Mime, 8, 12, 19–20
Monkey, 45
Moonwalk, 4, 6–9, 13, 17
Motown Records, 7

N

New York, 10–12, 16, 24, 26, 32, 39, 40, 44
New York Swing Dance Society, 41
New York Yankees, 29

O

Oprah Winfrey Show, The, 25

P

Philippines, 27
Pony, 45
Popping, 8, 20
Powers, Richard, 17

Q

Quadrille, 37

R

Ragtime, 15–17
Razor-Bey, Alyce, 33
Rhythm Universe, 33
Robot, 18–21, 25
Runnin' Wild, 35–36
Russell, Melinda, 28

S

San Francisco, 17, 20
Saturday Night Fever, 30–32
Savoy Ballroom, 39–41
Shields, Robert, 20
Silver, Ric, 24–25
Simpsons, The, 20
Snowden, George, 40
Solid Gold, 8
Soul Train, 19–20
South Carolina, 35–36
SpongeBob SquarePants, 20
Swing, 32, 39–41, 44

T

Thomas, Bob E., 36
Travolta, John, 31–32
Turkey trot, 14, 16–17
Twist, 42–45

U

United States, 23, 29, 32–33, 35–36

V

Vogue, 10–13, 17

W

Wailer, Bunny, 23
Waltz, 37
Whitey's Lindy Hoppers, 41

Y

Yankee Stadium, 29
Y.M.C.A., 47
Yoga, 11

What Do You Think?

1. Do you agree with our ranking? If you don't, try ranking these dances yourself. Justify your ranking with data from your own research and reasoning. You may refer to our criteria, or you may want to draw up your own list of criteria.

2. Here are three other dances that we considered but in the end did not include in our top 10 list: the chicken dance, the ketchup dance, and Y.M.C.A.
   - Find out more about these dances. Do you think they should have made our list? Give reasons for your response.
   - Are there other dances that you think should have made our list? Explain your choices.